Emma and the Mermaid Club

A MERMAID GIRLS CHAPTER BOOK

A.M. Luzzader

ILLUSTRATED BY
CHADD VANZANTEN

Published by Knowledge Forest Press
P.O. Box 6331
Logan, UT 84341

Ebook ISBN-13: 978-1-949078-67-1
Paperback ISBN-13: 978-1-949078-66-4

Cover design by Beautiful Book Covers (beetifulbookcovers.com)

Editing by Chadd VanZanten

Interior illustrations by Chadd VanZanten

For Lily, happy reading!

Contents

Chapter One

HUMANS AND MERMAIDS have lots of things in common. Mermaids go to school, just like humans do. Mermaids love their families and friends. They like to sing and dance and have fun.

But mermaids are different in some ways. Mermaids have tails and fins instead of legs and feet, of course. They swim instead of walking. They live in the ocean and breathe under water. They eat different foods, too. Merfolk do not eat hamburgers and milkshakes, but they do love clamburgers and kelpshakes.

Just like humans, each mermaid is unique. Also just like humans, every mermaid is special.

Many mermaids have long, wavy hair, but some

mermaids prefer short hair. All mermaid tails are colorful, but they are not all the same color. Mermaid tails can be orange, blue, purple, pink, green, or any other color. Some mermaid tails have many colors.

Some mermaids are curious. Some are funny. Some mermaids talk a lot, while others are quiet.

There are as many different mermaids as there are fish in the sea, and each one has a story. Mermaid stories are fun to read because the oceans are magical and full of adventure. All merfolk have a story to tell.

This story is about a mermaid named Emma Tailer and the Mermaid Club. Emma was a happy and smart mermaid, but in this story she has some challenges and learns some things about herself.

Emma had long, wavy brown hair and brown eyes. Her tail was orange, and when the sun was shining brightly, her scales glittered with pink and yellow. As you may already know, all merfolk are guardians of the sea. They promise to learn mermagic and protect sea life and the oceans.

Emma wasn't quite old enough to begin learning mermagic. Merfolk started magic lessons at around eleven years old. However, all merfolk knew a little mermagic.

Also, Emma already loved the ocean. She often swam up to the surface just to watch the sun sparkle on the waves.

One of Emma's favorite things was the ocean's many shades of blue. Blue was Emma's favorite color. At the surface of the sea, the water was greenish-blue and turquoise. Out in the open ocean, the water was a deep shade of blue. Way down at the bottom, the water was a color called indigo, a blue so dark that it was almost black. Swimming through the many kinds of blue in the sea made Emma's eyes grow wide with wonder.

Emma enjoyed collecting sea shells. She had a white and pink conch shell that took up nearly all the space on her bedside table. She had tiny cone snail shells, striped clam shells, and oyster shells that were rough on the outside but silky smooth and colorful on the inside.

Emma also loved reading about undersea adventures and stories about people on the land. Sometimes, Emma would be so excited about what was happening in her book, she'd even read all the way through lunch break.

One day, Emma was reading a book called, *The Adventures of Wilma the Whale*. She had come to the chapter when Wilma was captured by pirates. She'd been reading the book before and after school, and her teacher Ms. Seaside had even caught her reading it during math lesson.

"Emma," said Ms. Seaside.

"Yes, Ms. Seaside?" said Emma.

"Please put your book away during math class," said the teacher.

"Oh," said Emma. "Yes, ma'am. Sorry."

But Emma couldn't wait for math class to end so that she could read more. During recess, she didn't play red-rover swim-over with her friends Ava and Chloe.

Instead, Emma swam over to the tall sea grass at the edge of the playground. There she found a comfortable spot and propped herself up on the sandy ocean floor to read. Then she heard voices nearby.

Did someone say my name? Emma thought. She shook her head and kept reading.

Then Emma really did hear her name.

It's probably a different Emma. There are two other mermaids named Emma at the school, Emma thought. *There's Emma Seafoam and Emma Rae Prawn.*

Emma read her book, but she heard the voices again.

"Look at Emma all by herself," a mermaid said. "She is so shy!"

Emma lowered her book and listened closely. It was someone behind Emma, but she was too shy to turn around and look.

"Yeah," said a merboy, "Emma is as quiet as a clam."

They were talking about her! Emma felt her cheeks burning.

It was true. Emma wasn't very talkative. She wanted to get to know people before she spoke to them very much. Emma also liked being alone sometimes. She liked to be by herself to read and think.

Emma really was shy.

Being shy isn't a bad thing.

Being shy is just fine. Emma didn't know this yet.

Like I already told you, there were as many different mermaids as there are fish in the sea. All of them were unique and important in their own ways.

Emma knew that her wavy hair and sparkly tail were part of her. She knew her favorite color blue was part of her, too. Emma was smart and thoughtful. She loved to read and was very good at listening to others. That was Emma. But Emma didn't know that being shy was also part of her. She didn't know being shy made her unique and special.

And so when she heard the other merkids say she was shy, Emma felt embarrassed. She didn't want the other merkids to talk about her that way. She didn't want to be different. Emma tried to pretend she had not heard them.

I wish I was not so shy, she thought. *I should be more like Chloe and Ava.*

Chloe and Ava were Emma's two best friends. They weren't quiet and shy like Emma. In fact, you might say Chloe and Ava were both "un-shy." Un-shy is not a real word, of course. It was made up for this story. But it just means "not shy."

Emma's friend, Chloe, was very chatty. She had black hair and bright blue eyes. Her tail was light green. Chloe could talk to any merkid about anything. Chloe even talked to people she just met. Emma remembered one day when Chloe met a new merkid in class. The new merkid sat next to Chloe. His name was Tim Kelper.

"What do you like to eat for breakfast?" Chloe asked the new merkid. "I like sandcakes with maple sea-rup."

"I love sandcakes!" said Tim.

"Also, do you find dolphins rather strange?" asked Chloe. "Their voices are so squeaky!"

Chloe was talking to Tim Kelper as if they were old friends.

Ms. Seaside was sitting at her desk at the front of the classroom. "Chloe?" she called.

"Yes, Ms. Seaside?" said Chloe.

"Thank you for being so kind to Tim, our new student," said Ms. Seaside.

Chloe smiled and replied, "He's very nice!"

"Yes, Chloe, but there's a problem," said Ms. Seaside.

"Problem?" asked Chloe. "What problem?"

"Well, the whole class is taking a history test right now," said Ms. Seaside.

"Oh, right," said Chloe with a grin.

Chloe was so un-shy she often talked in class when she was supposed to be working.

"We'll talk later, Tim," whispered Chloe, picking up her pencil.

Emma's other best friend was Ava. Her hair and eyes were dark brown. Her tail shimmered purple and green. Ava was not as talkative as Chloe. Nobody was as talkative as Chloe. But Ava loved to be around lots of merfolk. She liked going to big picnics and noisy birthday parties, where everyone was laughing and playing.

Emma had trouble talking to people she just met. She got nervous in big crowds.

I should be more like Chloe and Ava, thought Emma. *I shouldn't be so shy all the time.* She closed her book. Then she went to find her friends so she could figure out how to be un-shy.

Chapter Two

"Emma! There you are!" cried Chloe.

Emma smiled. Chloe swam to Emma and gave her a big hug. Chloe's long, black hair waved in the water. Her green tail shimmered with sparkles of gold and blue.

"I've been looking for you!" said Chloe. "Where have you been, you silly fish?"

"Well, I—" Emma said.

Before Emma could answer, Chloe kept talking. This was something Chloe did. Chloe was so talkative, sometimes she just couldn't wait for someone else to answer. Ava did it sometimes, too. This happened a lot with Emma, because Emma was slow to answer. Emma also spoke quietly.

This didn't make Emma angry. She didn't mind when her friends spoke before she answered. Emma liked it when she didn't have to say much.

"I've started a club," Chloe said loudly. "It's called Mermaid Club!"

"What does the club do?" asked Emma.

"That's for the club to decide," said Chloe in a serious voice. "I know it will be fun. We'll meet new friends. We'll do fun things together. And we must also help others."

Emma didn't like big groups. She got nervous when meeting new friends. She didn't like talking very much, either.

Wait! Emma suddenly thought. *This is perfect! Mermaid Club will help me to be un-shy!*

"May I join Mermaid Club?"

"Yes, of course!" cried Chloe. "Mermaid Club is for anyone who wants to join!"

"How many members are there so far?"

"So far?" said Chloe. She tapped her cheek with her finger. "So far, there are only three members. Me, Ava, and you."

"That sounds perfect," said Emma.

"No, we have to find more members," said Chloe. "I want this to be a big club! No one should feel left out. We must ask everyone in class if they want to join."

"Everyone?" asked Emma nervously.

"Yes, everyone," replied Chloe. "It's okay if they say no, but we must ask everyone. Will you help me do that?"

Emma did not like the idea. She would have to swim up to kids she did not know very well. She would have to talk to them. She knew, though, that this was a way to be more like Chloe and Ava. She knew this would help her be more outgoing.

And so Emma said, "Yes, of course I'll help."

Emma wished there was another way to help. She really wanted to help, but she was nervous.

"Thank you!" said Chloe. "Look! There's Nevaeh over there."

Emma looked and saw Nevaeh, a mermaid with orange and yellow hair and blue eyes. Emma didn't know Nevaeh very well.

"You go ask Nevaeh if she would like to join Mermaid Club," said Chloe. "I'll ask Paul."

"Um, okay," said Emma.

Chloe swam over to Paul and began talking with him right away. Emma heard Chloe ask Paul about Mermaid Club. It was so easy for Chloe to talk to anyone about anything! As Emma began swimming in Nevaeh's direction, her heart began to beat faster.

It's not a big deal, Emma told herself. *Stop being shy!*

As Emma came closer, Nevaeh turned and said, "Hi, Emma."

Even though Emma was a mermaid who lived in the sea, her mouth felt dry. And she had trouble breathing. And her stomach felt like it was full of wild jellyfish.

"Oh, um, hi!" said Emma. She meant to say, "Hi, Nevaeh," but suddenly, Emma could not remember Nevaeh's name!

This happened to Emma when she felt especially shy and nervous. She forgot names. Sometimes Emma would even forget her own name.

"What's up?" asked Nevaeh.

Emma thought hard and remembered Nevaeh's name. "Um, hi, Nevaeh!" said Emma. "I want to ask—I mean talk—I mean ask—about Chloe Club."

"Huh?" said Nevaeh.

Emma was so nervous, her words came out wrong! This was something else that happened when Emma got nervous or upset. She got mixed up and said silly things.

"I meant to say Clermaid Mub!" said Emma. Her face turned red.

"What's that?" asked Nevaeh.

Emma said, "Um, Chloe started a thing!"

"What kind of thing?" said Nevaeh.

"I don't know!" cried Emma. And she was so upset, she hurried away without another word.

Emma swam to the edge of the playground. She

left a cloud of nervous bubbles behind her. Emma swam through the tall sea grass waving at the edge of the playground. She was so upset, she didn't pay attention to where she was swimming.

A passing school of silver sardines suddenly swam all around her. A "school" of sardines isn't like a school for learning. Sardines and other fish traveled together, and their groups are called "schools." They all went the same direction. They all turned and circled the same way. They were small, but there were thousands of them. Emma had to swim with them. She had no choice. Their silver scales flashed like mirrors in the sun. She couldn't find her way out, so she swam where they swam.

"I'm sure recess is over!" Emma said to herself as she went along with the sardines. "I'll be late for class!"

When she finally got away from the sardines, she found herself in the deep part of the sea. It was dark and a little scary.

"This is all my fault because I'm so shy!" Emma whimpered to herself.

Emma felt very sad and afraid, and it was a long time before she found her way back to her school.

Chapter Three

By the time Emma got to her school, she really was late for class. She tried to explain to Ms. Seaside what had happened, but it wasn't easy. Emma was worried that Ms. Seaside would scold her.

"I was talking to Nevaeh—Chloe has a thing," said Emma. She was very upset. "But then the sardines—I got lost—" Emma was getting her words mixed up again.

Ms. Seaside was very patient. She didn't understand what Emma was trying to tell her, but she got the general idea. She said, "It's okay, Emma. Take a deep breath. You've had a bad time, haven't you?"

Emma nodded. Then she took a deep breath of ocean water. It was a mermagical trick all merfolk knew. Taking a deep breath made them calm down and think more clearly. Emma had forgotten about it. She breathed in and out. The mermagic calmed her down.

"It's reading time, as you know," said Ms. Seaside. "I think the quiet will also make you feel better. Take your seat and everything will be all right."

The classroom was very quiet. The other merkids were all reading their books. They didn't notice Emma. No one looked at Emma or spoke to her. She liked that.

Emma just wanted to keep to herself for a while. She sat down and opened her book. Just as Ms. Seaside had said, Emma soon felt much better.

After school, however, Chloe said it was time to hold the first meeting of Mermaid Club. So far, there were still only three members of the club—Chloe, Emma, and Ava. Emma felt slightly nervous about the meeting. The three friends gathered on the sandy playground for the meeting.

"Emma," said Chloe. "Did you ask Nevaeh to join the club?"

"Yeah, kinda," Emma mumbled.

"What did she say?" asked Chloe.

"I'm not sure," she said softly.

"Do you mean she wants to think about it?" said Chloe.

"Yeah, maybe," said Emma, her voice still quiet.

Chloe told them she had invited Paul, Kate, and Mia.

"Paul said he might join," said Chloe. "Kate said no thanks. Mia said she will join, but she couldn't come to the meeting today."

"I asked two of my friends," said Ava. "They said they will come to our next meeting."

"Fintastic!" said Chloe. "We are off to a good start! Let's get more members. This will be a fun group for everyone who joins."

Emma nodded, but she secretly hoped not too many people would join. She also hoped that she wouldn't have to invite anyone else to join.

"Now we must elect officers for Mermaid Club," said Chloe in her serious voice. "The officers will keep the club running."

Emma and Ava nodded.

"First, we need a club president," said Chloe. "The president will be in charge of meetings. The president will also plan our fun activities."

"You should be president," Ava said to Chloe, "since it was your idea."

"No, we must vote," said Chloe. "We must be fair. Does anyone else want to be president?"

Ava turned to Emma and asked, "Emma, would you like to be president?"

Emma's eyes grew wide with fright, and she shook her head.

"Then I vote for Chloe to be president of Mermaid Club," said Ava, raising her hand.

Emma raised her hand and quietly said, "I vote for Chloe, too."

"Very well," said Chloe. "I will be president. Thank you for your votes. I will plan fun things to do and make sure everyone feels welcome."

Emma smiled and nodded. *Chloe will be a very good club president,* she thought.

"The next officer we need is a vice president," said Chloe. "The vice president will be in charge if the president is absent. You know, like if I have homework to do, or if my family goes to visit my aunt."

Emma did not want to be vice president. She wanted to help out in Mermaid Club, but she did not want to be in charge or swim up in front of everyone, even if it were only when the president was away.

"I think I would like to be vice president," said Ava.

Emma was glad when Ava volunteered to be the vice president.

"You have my vote, Ava," said Chloe, raising her hand.

Emma raised her hand. "I vote for Ava, too," she said in her quiet voice.

"Great," said Chloe. "We have a president and vice president. We can begin to plan what Mermaid Club will do. Does anyone have any ideas for fun activities?"

"We could go to the sea horse races," said Ava. "Or we could go to the sand castle contest."

Both of those ideas sounded okay to Emma, but

she knew there would be lots of noise and merfolk. Emma preferred small, quiet gatherings.

"Those sound very fun!" said Chloe. "When are the sea horse races?"

"A few weeks from now," said Ava.

"Hm," said Chloe. "That's a long time. When is the sand castle contest?"

"Next month," said Ava.

"Ava, those are great ideas," said Chloe. "Is there something we can do sooner?"

Emma had an idea, but she raised her hand so shyly, Chloe and Ava didn't notice. So she waved her hand a little to get their attention.

"Do you have an idea, Emma?" asked Chloe.

"Yes. Didn't you say the club would also do nice things to help merfolks in the community?"

"Yes, we should," said Chloe.

"Well," said Emma, "Ms. Seaside once told me that Sunny Oceans Senior Living Center likes it when merkids come to visit the senior merfolk. Some of them are lonely."

Sunshine Oceans Senior Living Center was a home for older mermaids and mermen who weren't able to live by themselves. They needed nurses and helpers. Emma's grandmother had lived at Sunny

Oceans Living Center before she passed away. Her grandmother had always loved visitors.

"That's a great idea!" said Ava.

"Yes, it's perfect," said Chloe. "Let's plan to go there after school on Friday! I'll ask them if it's okay for us to visit."

Emma was very glad. She liked to visit Sunshine Oceans Senior Living Center. She loved how quiet it was. She would have a quiet talk with one of the senior merfolks. Or they might work on a puzzle or go for a short swim.

"Oh, I almost forgot!" said Chloe. "We need one more officer. Emma, will you be our membership officer?"

Emma thought the membership officer would write down the names of the members of the club. Or maybe the membership officer would take the roll at the meetings. Either way, it sounded good to Emma, because she could do it quietly and without talking too much.

"Sure," Emma said softly. "I'd love to be the membership officer."

"Then I vote for Emma," said Chloe. She raised her hand.

Ava raised her hand, too. "I vote for Emma!"

"Emma," said Chloe, "you are the Mermaid Club membership officer. Your job is to talk to people about joining Mermaid Club."

"Wait, what?" cried Emma, suddenly sitting up very straight. She wore a frightened look on her face.

"Don't worry," said Chloe. "I'll give you a long list of people to invite. You'll have so much fun!"

Chapter Four

WHEN EMMA GOT HOME, she moped into her room and flopped onto her bed. Her job was to talk to other merkids about Mermaid Club. Emma was supposed to go around and invite new members.

But she didn't want to.

So, she lay on her bed and sighed. Then fed her pet goldfish, Benny. She watched Benny swim around the room, eating his little fish flakes.

Next, Emma looked at every shell in her seashell collection. She decided to move her big conch shell to the bookcase and put some fancy whelk shells on her bedside table. Then she switched them back.

Emma sighed again. She really did not want to

invite new members to Mermaid Club. It made her uneasy just thinking about it.

I think I'd rather do three hours of homework! she thought. Then Emma had a great idea. *That's it! Instead of inviting the merkids on my list, I'll do all my homework!*

But she had finished all her homework at school. There was no homework to work on. She sighed again.

Mermaid Club was supposed to make me less shy, she thought. *But it's not working at all.*

Her mother, Rebecca, swam past her door.

"Oh hi, Emma!" called Rebecca. "How was school?"

"Fine," said Emma quietly.

"Fine" was a word that Emma sometimes used when everything was not "fine." The day had not been all bad. There had been good parts of the day, like when she found out she got a good score on her math test. Joining the Mermaid Club and talking with Ava and Chloe had been good, too.

But there were also parts of the day that Emma didn't like—like when those merkids on the playground called Emma shy. She had also run away from Nevaeh, gotten lost, and been late for class. That wasn't "fine." Then she had been voted to be membership officer of Mermaid Club. That wasn't very "fine" at all.

Rebecca must have known something was wrong. She swam into the bedroom and sat down on the bed next to Emma.

"Hey, Emma," said her mother. "It seems like your energy might be a little low. Are you feeling down? Is there anything you'd like to talk about?"

Emma wasn't sure she could explain what she was feeling. "I joined a club today. Chloe started it. It's called Mermaid Club. She's the president and Ava is vice president."

"That sounds fun," Rebecca said.

"Yeah," said Emma in her quiet voice.

"So, what's wrong, sweetie?" Rebecca asked. "Did you want to be the president?"

"Oh my goodness, no!" said Emma.

"Oh," said Rebecca, "you wanted to be the vice president?"

"No way," replied Emma. "I'm the membership officer."

"Well, that's terrific, honey," said Rebecca.

"No," said Emma, "it's terrible. I have to talk to everyone in class and ask them if they want to join the club."

"Oooh," said Rebecca. "So, you're worried about having to talk to all those students? You're afraid to talk to merkids whom you don't know very well?"

"Yes!" cried Emma.

"You don't have to do anything you don't want to," said Emma's mother. "You know that, right?"

"Sure," said Emma. "But I joined Mermaid Club so that I can be un-shy, like Chloe and Ava, but instead it's making me more shy!"

"I see," said Rebecca. "Why do you think you need to be un-shy?"

"I don't know," explained Emma. "I guess it's because some kids on the playground teased me for being so shy. They said I was quiet as a clam! I was so embarrassed!"

"Well," said Rebecca, "'Shy' and 'quiet' are just words. You are a mermaid, and you should never be embarrassed about who you are. You know that."

"Don't you think I need to be talkative and outgoing, like Chloe and Ava?" Emma asked.

"The ocean already has a Chloe and an Ava,"

Rebecca said. "Both of them are lovely and unique. Do you agree?"

Emma quickly nodded.

"But, Emma," said her mother, "the ocean needs all kinds of merfolk, and that includes you!"

Emma blinked, then looked up at her mother. "You mean it's okay for me to be this way?" she asked. "It's okay if I'm quiet and nervous around merfolk that I don't know? It's okay if I like to be by myself?"

Emma's mother smiled and said, "Absolutely."

Chapter Five

It was Friday, the day that Mermaid Club planned to visit the Sunshine Oceans Senior Living Center. Chloe, Ava, and Emma met up after school to get ready for the trip.

"Emma," asked Chloe, "have you invited anyone else to join us?"

"No," said Emma. "I've been a little busy."

This was Emma's way of saying she was too nervous to be membership officer. Emma planned to tell this to Chloe after they went to visit Sunshine Oceans Senior Living Center

"That's okay," said Chloe. "Paul and Mia have joined."

"Yes," said Ava. "And my friends, Luke and Christi, have joined.

Emma was happy to hear this. When all the new members had arrived, Chloe led them to the Sunshine Oceans Senior Living Center.

A grown-up mermaid who worked for the senior center met them at the entrance. She had short, red hair and matching glasses.

"My name is Stacy Shoal," she said. "Thank you so much for visiting our center. Our residents love to have visitors! Right now they're in the community room. You and the residents can pick what you'd like to do. We have lots of games, puzzles, and musical instruments."

Emma and the other Mermaid Club members swam into the community room. Emma noticed that the water in the room was pleasantly warm and that there were plenty of sea plants for decoration. All over the room there were older merfolk who had wrinkled faces and graying hair. The scales on their tails weren't as sparkly as younger mers, but Emma thought they all looked very nice.

Emma felt a little nervous about speaking to the residents. She didn't know any of them, yet. Emma didn't like starting conversations with people she didn't know well. She started to feel a little bad, thinking she was being shy again, but then she thought, *No, it's okay to feel a little nervous meeting someone new.* She took a deep breath of seawater. The mermagical trick made her a little calmer.

Emma glanced around the room. She looked for something she might talk about with one of the residents. Like sea shells or books. She didn't see any seashell collections like the one she had at home. Then she spotted an older mermaid who had silver hair and a dark blue tail. She was sitting on a chair and in her lap was a copy of *The Adventures of Wilma the Whale.*

It was the very same book that Emma had been reading! Emma swam over to the mermaid.

She still felt a little nervous, but it helped to have something to talk about.

"Hi, I'm Emma," she said. "Are you enjoying that book?"

The older mermaid looked up from the book. She smiled in a way that made Emma think she was happy to see her.

"Hello, Emma," said the mermaid. "I'm Patty.

Yes! I'm enjoying this book, but my eyes are not as good as they used to be. Sometimes it's hard for me to read the words."

"I'm reading that book, too!" said Emma. "Would you like me to read to you?"

"Yes, please," said Patty.

Emma sat down next to Patty and read from the book. After they read for a while, Patty and Emma talked about what they liked about the book and what they didn't like. Emma was glad she had joined the Mermaid Club and that they had come to the Sunshine Oceans Senior Living Center because Patty had become her newest friend.

While they were talking, Emma heard harsh voices and yelling in the room. Emma looked around and saw an older merman who seemed very angry.

"No! No!" he shouted. "Get away! Leave me alone!"

Emma saw Chloe and Ava there, too.

There was a big problem with Mermaid Club.

Chapter Six

"Patty," said Emma. "Will you excuse me? I'd like to see if I can help with the trouble over there."

"Yes, dear," said Patty. "Go and see what's wrong. Mr. McSalty is angry and shouting. He sometimes loses his temper."

Emma set down the book and swam over to Chloe and Ava. Mr. McSalty was sitting in a swimchair. He couldn't swim by himself anymore and needed a swimchair to get around. It was a little like a wheelchair, but instead of wheels, it had a little propeller to make it go. Mr. McSalty sat in the swimchair with an angry look on his face.

"What's the matter?" Emma asked Chloe.

"I don't know," said Chloe.

Emma could tell Chloe and Ava didn't know what to do.

"What would you like to do?" Chloe asked Mr. McSalty.

Mr. McSalty said, "I want—I want to—"

But Chloe didn't let him finish. "You want to put together a puzzle?"

"No!" grumbled Mr. McSalty.

"You want us to take you outside for a swim?" asked Ava.

"No! No!" said the old merman. He spoke slowly. "What I want is—"

"A snack?" asked Chloe. "Some tuna chips? How about some fish fries?"

"No!" snarled Mr. McSalty. And he pulled the lever on this swimchair. The propeller started to whirl, and Mr. McSalty zipped out of the community room.

Chloe and Ava swam after him, shouting, "Come back, Mr. McSalty! I'm sorry! What's wrong?"

Mr. McSalty swam his chair out into the courtyard outside. Chloe and Ava swam after him, but Mr. McSalty's swimchair was fast! He zoomed back into the community room at a high speed. He knocked over a potted sea plant. He knocked over a table and ruined the puzzle some of the other residents were putting together.

"Mr. McSalty!" yelled Chloe. "Come back! Let us help you!"

Emma watched as Mr. McSalty swam round and round the room. He went up and down, side to side, and in circles. Everyone ducked out of his way. Mr. McSalty swam around so fast he started a whirlpool in the room. Books and puzzle pieces swirled everywhere.

Stacy Shoals swam into the room. "What's going on?" she cried.

Chloe and Ava swam over to Stacy Shoals. They were very tired from trying to catch Mr. McSalty. Mr. McSalty stopped his swimchair over in a corner. He sat with arms folded and his back to everyone else.

"We're not sure what went wrong, Ms. Shoals," said Chloe, breathing hard. "Mr. McSalty got upset and swam his swimchair all over the room!"

"I see," said Stacy Shoals. "Let me explain. Mr. McShoals is a very private and quiet gentlemer. He's sometimes nervous around merfolk whom he doesn't know. Sometimes, strangers make him cranky."

He's quiet? thought Emma. *And he feels nervous like I do? And Chloe was answering before he could speak? I think I know what's wrong!*

Emma tried to speak up as boldly as she could. "Ms. Shoals," she said. "May I talk to Mr. McSalty? I'll try not to upset him anymore."

"Yes," said Stacy Shoals. "Please give it a try."

Emma swam over and stood next to Mr. McSalty, but not too close. She took another deep breath. The mermagical trick made her feel calmer.

"Pardon me, sir," she said. "My name is Emma."

"What do you want?" grumbled Mr. McSalty.

"I'm sorry my friends upset you," she said. "They're very nice but also very talkative. Sometimes they talk more than they listen. May I help?"

"Well, missy," said Mr. McSalty in a grumpy voice. "Believe it or not, I was glad when the Mermaid Club came to visit. I really was."

Emma said nothing. She just listened.

"In fact," Mr. McSalty said, "I was hoping Miss Chloe and Miss Ava would play a game with me. I love games. Crabble is my favorite game."

Emma liked to play Crabble, too, but she knew it wasn't the right time to say that. She only nodded and kept listening.

Mr. McSalty continued, but he didn't sound angry anymore. "It's my glasses. That's the problem. I can't see a thing without my glasses. I can't play Crabble without them."

Emma saw that Mr. McSalty was not wearing glasses. She guessed that he had dropped his glasses or left them behind somewhere. She could have said this, but she just kept listening.

"Well, I can't find them," he said sadly. "I can't find my glasses. Maybe I left them in my room. Or maybe I dropped them. I don't know. I tried to tell Miss Ava and Miss Chloe, but there was so much noise and so many merkids around. I guess I got a little uneasy, and I lost my temper. I feel embarrassed now."

"I get uneasy when in big, noisy groups, too," said Emma.

"You do?" he asked.

"Yep," she answered. "But it's okay. Let's look for your glasses."

"Thank you, Miss Emma," said Mr. McSalty.

Everyone joined together to find Mr. McSalty's glasses. But the community room was a total shipwreck. Books and tuna chips floated around. Potted sea plants were dumped over. Chairs lay on their sides.

"What a mess!" said Emma.

"Oh," said Mr. McSalty. "I hope my glasses are not lost or broken!"

The merkids and residents straightened the room as they looked for Mr. McSalty's glasses.

Then Chloe cried out, "Mr. McSalty! Are these your glasses?"

Mr. McSalty swam his swimchair over to Chloe.

"Yes!" he said with a laugh. "Those are my glasses! You found them! Thank you!"

Chloe handed the glasses to Mr. McSalty. He put them on.

"That's much better," he said, blinking. "Now can we play a game of Crabble?"

"Yes!" said the Mermaid Club all together.

Patty came over to play. She was friends with Mr. McSalty. Paul and Christi also wanted to play Crabble.

Chloe pulled Emma aside. She said, "Emma! You saved Mermaid Club. Without you, our first activity would have been ruined!"

"I'm glad I could help," Emma said.

"Let me ask you a question," said Chloe. "Do you really want to be membership officer?"

Emma almost said, "Yes," because then she wouldn't have to say anything else. She felt embarrassed that the job was not right for her. Instead, Emma sighed and said, "To be honest, no. I don't want to be the membership officer."

"You like listening to people more than you like talking to people," said Chloe. "Is that why?"

"Oh, yes," said Emma, glad that Chloe understood.

Emma was very glad she was in Mermaid Club. She didn't talk as much as Chloe. She didn't like big groups like Ava did. But that was okay. Like Chloe said, Mermaid Club was for everyone, even mermaids who were quiet.

Chloe said, "Emma, you are really good at listening to others and paying attention to how people feel."

Ava came over. "What's going on?" she said.

Chloe said, "I think Emma needs a different job in Mermaid Club."

"Oh?" said Emma nervously. "What job?"

"I think you should be Mermaid Club's secretary," said Chloe. "You will listen and pay attention to our meetings and activities. You will take notes and help us solve problems with your listening skills."

"I would love to do that job," said Emma. "May I vote for myself?"

Chloe and Ava laughed.

"Of course!" cried Chloe. "All in favor, raise your hands!"

They all raised their hands.

Please leave a review

~~~

Thank you for reading this book. I hope you enjoyed it! I would really appreciate it if you would please take a moment to review Emma and the Mermaid Club at the retail site where it was purchased. This helps me to reach new readers. Thank you!

—A.M. Luzzader

WWW.AMLUZZADER.COM

- blog
- freebies
- newsletter
- contact info

About the Author

A.M. Luzzader is an award-winning children's book author who writes chapter books and middle grade books. She specializes in writing books for preteens including *A Mermaid in Middle Grade and Arthur Blackwood's Scary Stories for Kids who Like Scary Stories*

A.M. decided she wanted to write fun stories for

kids when she was still a kid herself. By the time she was in fourth grade, she was already writing short stories. In fifth grade, she bought a typewriter at a garage sale to put her words into print, and in sixth grade she added illustrations.

Now that she has decided what she wants to be when she grows up, A.M. writes books for kids full time. She was selected as the Writer of the Year in 2019-2020 by the League of Utah Writers.

A.M. is the mother of a 12-year-old and a 15-year-old who often inspire her stories. She lives with her husband and children in northern Utah. She is a devout cat person and avid reader.

A.M. Luzzader's books are appropriate for ages 5-12. Her chapter books are intended for kindergarten to third grade, and her middle grade books are for third grade through sixth grade. Find out more about A.M., sign up to receive her newsletter, and get special offers at her website: www.amluzzader.com.

facebook.com/a.m.luzzader

instagram.com/amluzzader

OTHER BOOKS BY
A.M. Luzzader

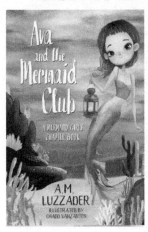 

Mermaid Club: A mermaid girls chapter book

For ages 6-10

OTHER BOOKS BY
A.M. Luzzader

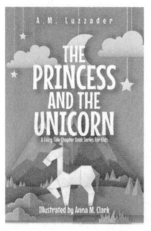 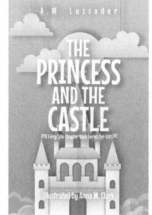

A Fairy Tale Chapter Book Series for Kids

For ages
6-10

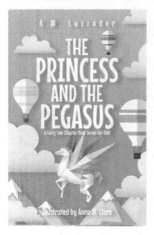 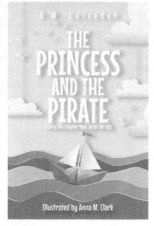
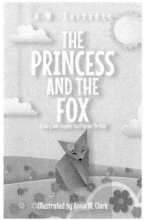

OTHER BOOKS BY
A.M. Luzzader

A Magic School for Girls Chapter Book

For ages 6-8

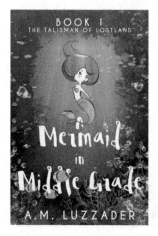 

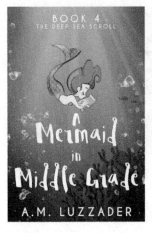 

A Mermaid in Middle Grade
Books 4-6

For ages
8-12